Beyond the Castle Walls

by Deb Martin
Illustrated by April D'Angelo

This Book Belongs To:

Library of Congress Control Number: 2006924811

This book is dedicated with love to my wonderful children:

Brandon Scott Martin
whose compassion and courage make him my hero

and

Brooke Christine Martin
whose beauty on the outside runs as deep on the inside

ver the hills
in Lancaster Land
lives a beautiful princess
in a castle so grand.

Dutch Wonderland is the name
of the Kingdom she graces,
and this Kingdom is one
of the most special places.

It's A Kingdom For Kids,
with rides, games and shows,
and new reasons to smile
every time that you go.

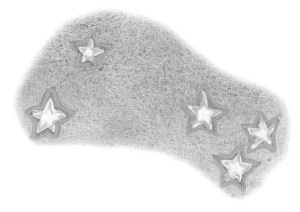

This is a story
about Princess Brooke,
and her amazing adventures
on the journey she took!

Of course, Princess Brooke
never travels alone,
so she brought Duke the Dragon
to explore the unknown.

Duke is friendly and purple.
He loves hugs and high fives.
How will you wave to Duke
when you see him outside?

A knight from the castle
then joined these two.
There is safety in numbers,
that much they knew!

His name is Sir Brandon.
He is brave and quite tall.
As an expert in safety,
he'd watch over them all.

So off they all went
on a worldwide trek,
with Duke carrying luggage
piled up to his neck!

They wanted to see countries
and cultures of all kinds,
and meet the princesses of the world –
as many as they could find.

They went to Australia,
a land called "Down Under,"
where the fish in the seas
filled them with wonder.

The Australian princess said, "G'day,"
which means hello to me and you.
An Aboriginal native welcomed them
by playing his didgeridoo.

The koala bears are oh-so-cute
in the eucalyptus trees,
and the kangaroos jump really high.
Would you try jumping, please?

They visited China;
there was so much to do!
Sir Brandon got a kick
out of learning Kung Fu.

China is a huge country
so many people live there.
It is also quite famous
for its giant panda bears.

Pandas live in the mountains
among the bamboo.
They even climb trees.
Can you pretend to climb, too?

When they saw a princess in a kimono
carrying a folded paper fan,
they knew that they had come
to the country called Japan!

The princess taught them origami,
making paper into shapes.
They made an origami dragon
that had Duke the Dragon's face!

Japan has lovely gardens with ponds,
where giant goldfish splash and splish.
Can you make your mouth like an "O"
and pretend you are a fish?

They spent lots of time in Russia,
a country far and wide.
It's the biggest country in the world,
when you measure Russia's size.

The princess wore a fur hood,
since Russian winters are very cold.
They took sleigh rides to wintry palaces
with turrets painted gold.

They toured ancient cathedrals
and food markets in little towns.
They clapped for the Russian ballet
and famous circus clowns.

They visited princesses in Europe,
a continent that isn't very big.
They did a German polka,
and danced an Irish jig.

They ate pizza in Italy;
in England, fish and chips;
and Switzerland's cheese
had them smacking their lips!

They smelled perfume in France
and tulips in Holland one day.
In Spain, Duke did a Flamenco dance!
Can you yell, "Ole!"?

Their next stop was Africa,
with so many sights to tour.
From Egypt to Botswana –
over 30 countries to explore!

They met princesses with dresses
that were colorful and bright.
They rode camels in the deserts,
and climbed mountains of great heights.

There were rainforests and jungles
with animals of every size.
On safari, lions roared
and zebras leaped before their eyes!

An elephant gave Duke a ride
with his trunk swinging high and low.
Can you use your arms
and swing them to and fro?

Then on to South America,
a continent with quite a history.
They explored age-old ruins
for clues to ancient mysteries.

They met princesses in Chile,
Columbia and Argentina, too.
In Venezuela they picked cocoa beans,
and climbed mountains in Peru.

In Brazil they sailed the Amazon,
a river famous for its size.
In the rainforest, playful monkeys
swung from trees that were so high.

They met princesses in India,
Pakistan and Saudi Arabia.
They went to Turkey and Afghanistan,
to Israel and Malaysia.

They traveled the world.
All the countries they explored!
They learned so many things
they had not known before.

When it was time to go home,
Princess Brooke grew concerned.
"How can we share with kids everywhere
all the things that we've learned?"

They invited each princess
to visit Dutch Wonderland.
Princess Brooke wrote them all notes
for Sir Brandon to deliver by hand.

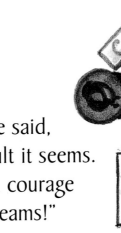

"I'll deliver them all," he said,
"no matter how difficult it seems.
It takes hard work and courage
to accomplish your dreams!"

While he traveled, he stayed safe
by remembering these tips:
Watch where you're going
because you don't want to trip!

When going over a train track
that doesn't have a gate,
stop, look and listen –
remember to wait!

Sir Brandon walked a lot
with different traffic to get through.
He looked both ways when crossing.
I hope that you do, too!

He delivered a note
to each princess by hand.
Every one said they'd come
and visit Dutch Wonderland.

Princess Brooke shared her Kingdom
with her new friends so dear,
and said, "You're all Princesses
of Dutch Wonderland while you're here."

And when their travels
sometimes keep them apart,
they remember the friendships
they keep in their hearts.

So even though you may not have
a castle to share,
there are still many ways
to show others you care.

Just give them a smile.
It's so easy to do.
The next thing you know,
they will smile back at you!

Also learn how to read
and keep books by your side.
Your imagination will take YOU
on travels worldwide!

So share and read
and be filled with laughter.
Our wish is that you will live
Dutch Wonderfully ever after!

About the Author and Illustrator

Deb Martin has a bachelor's degree in elementary education from BIOLA University, La Mirada, CA. As Director of Entertainment & Marketing for Dutch Wonderland, Deb still enjoys having a connection with young children. Deb is the proud mom of two grown children, Brandon and Brooke. Her most prized gift is her Himalayan cat, Kashi, given to her by a guest from Japan that she hosted in her home for a year.

April D'Angelo has a Bachelor of Fine Arts from Moore College of Art, Philadelphia, PA. She works in a variety of media. She exhibits her paintings in local art shows such as Yellow Springs, The Artists Circle, Flying Colors and most recently, The Philadelphia Sketch Club. April's portraits of children, adults and pets hang in numerous private homes. Each year she runs a summer art program for children. To learn more, visit her website: artbyapril.com